Denise Fleming

Go, Shapes, Go!

BEACH LANE BOOKS

New York London Toronto Sydney New Delhi

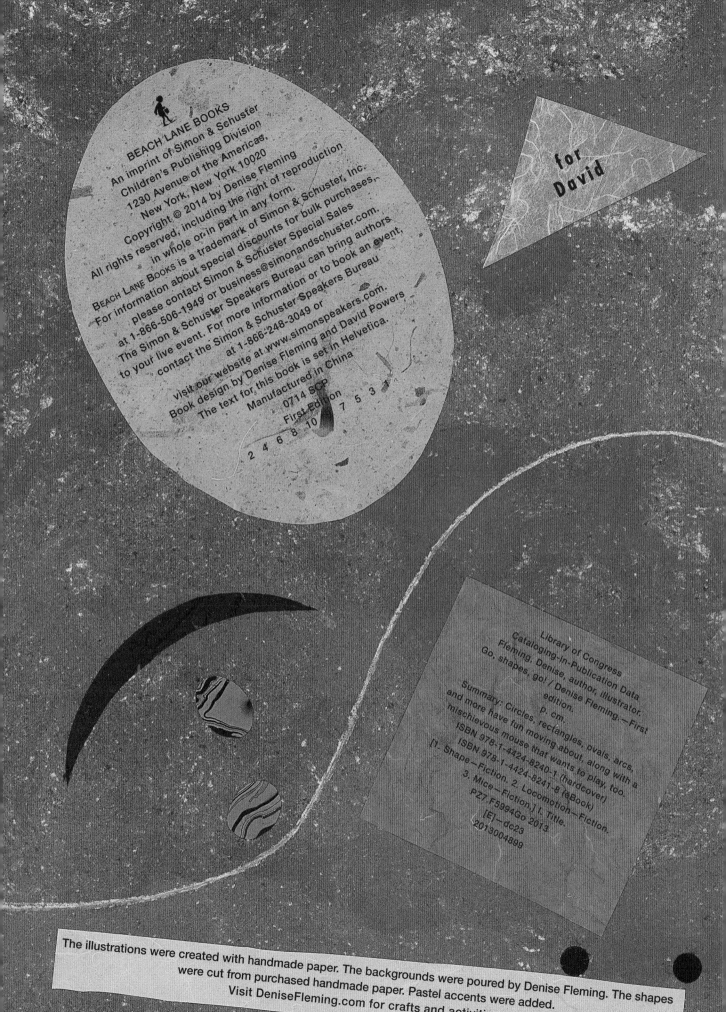

BEACH LANE BOOKS
An imprint of Simon & Schuster
Children's Publishing Division
1230 Avenue of the Americas,
New York, New York 10020
Copyright © 2014 by Denise Fleming
All rights reserved, including the right of reproduction
in whole or in part in any form.
BEACH LANE BOOKS is a trademark of Simon & Schuster, Inc.
For information about special discounts for bulk purchases,
please contact Simon & Schuster Special Sales
at 1-866-506-1949 or business@simonandschuster.com.
The Simon & Schuster Speakers Bureau can bring authors
to your live event. For more information or to book an event,
contact the Simon & Schuster Speakers Bureau
at 1-866-248-3049 or
visit our website at www.simonspeakers.com.
Book design by Denise Fleming and David Powers
The text for this book is set in Helvetica.
Manufactured in China
0714 SCP
First Edition
2 4 6 8 10 7 5 3 1

SHAPES are in place
and ready to go!

triangle

small arc

arc

circle

oval

small ovals

tiny circles

big rectangles

thin rectangles

half circles

Slide, SQUARE,
and start the show!

triangle

small arc

arc

circle

small
ovals

tiny
circles

big rectangles

thin rectangles

half circles

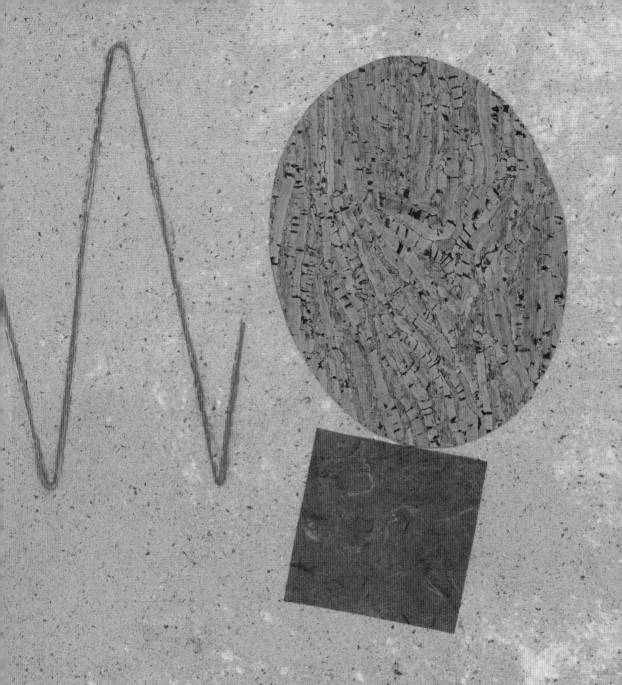

Bounce, OVAL,
up and down.

small arc

triangle

arc

small ovals

big rectangles

thin rectangles

tiny circles

half circles

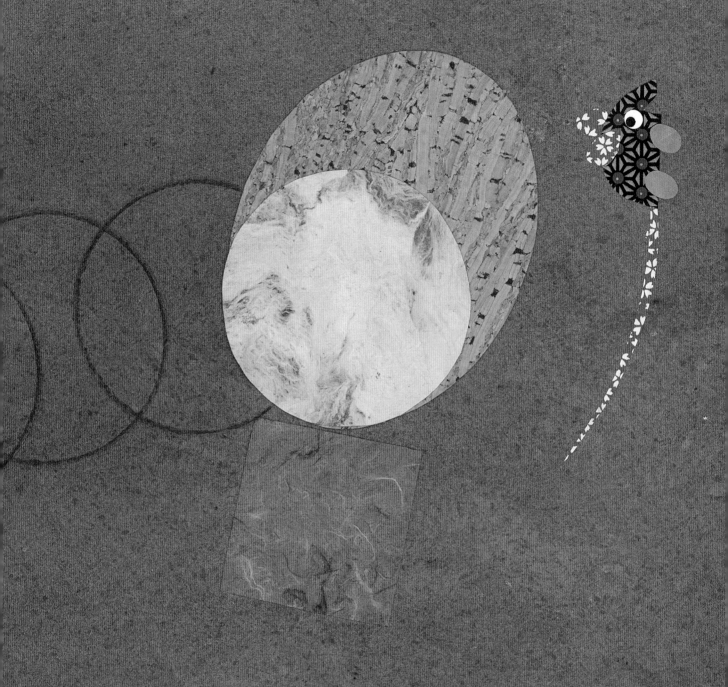

Roll, CIRCLE,

round and round.

small arc

small oval

thin rectangles

triangle

big rectangles

half circles

small oval

tiny circles

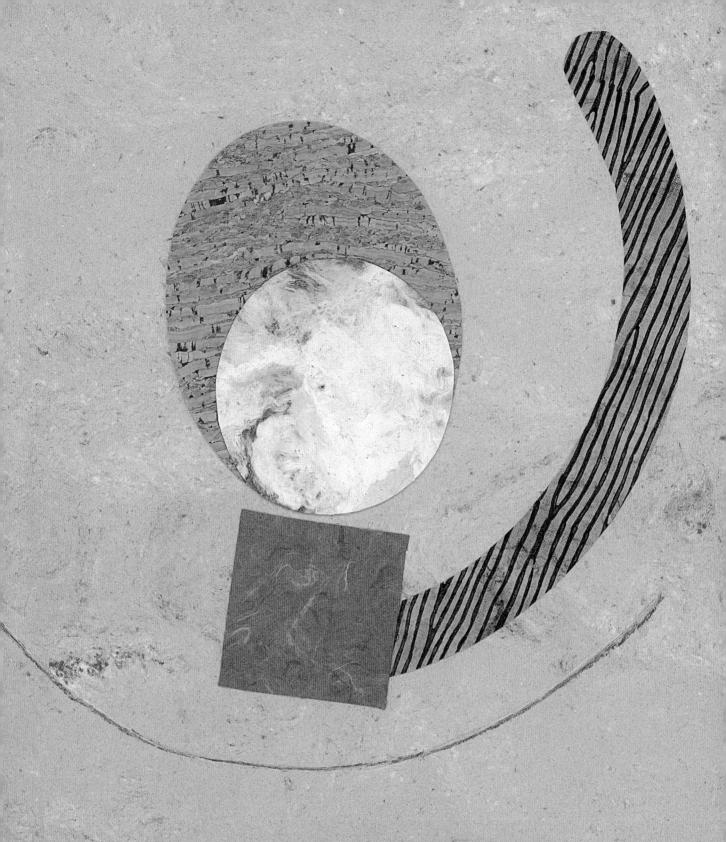

Slither, ARC,
like a snake.

Flip,
thin RECTANGLES.

Don't break!

small arc

small ovals

big rectangles

triangle

half circles

tiny circles

March,
big RECTANGLES.

One, two. One, two.

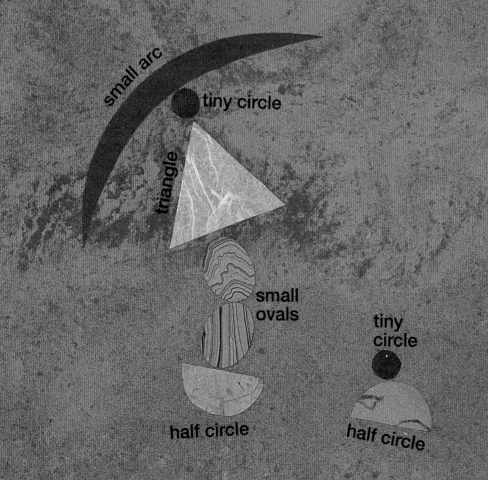

small arc

tiny circle

triangle

small
ovals

tiny
circle

half circle

half circle

Leap, half CIRCLES.

Look at you!

triangle

small
ovals

small arc

tiny
circles

Scoot, small OVALS.
My, oh my!

small arc

triangle

tiny circles

Fly, tiny CIRCLES,
way up high.

triangle

small arc

Twirl, small ARC.

Bibbity bop!

triangle

Hop, TRIANGLE,
to the top!

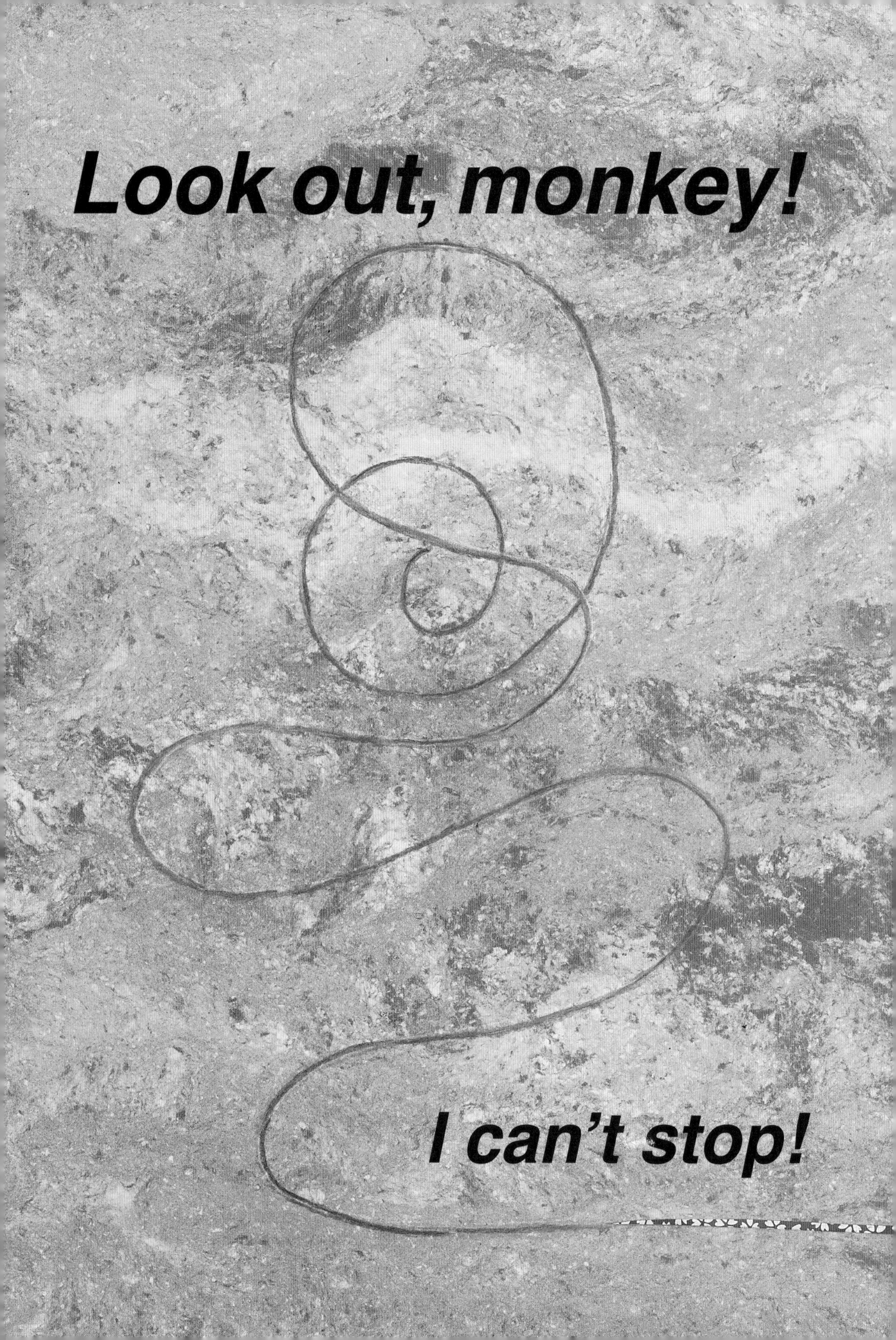

Look out, monkey!

I can't stop!

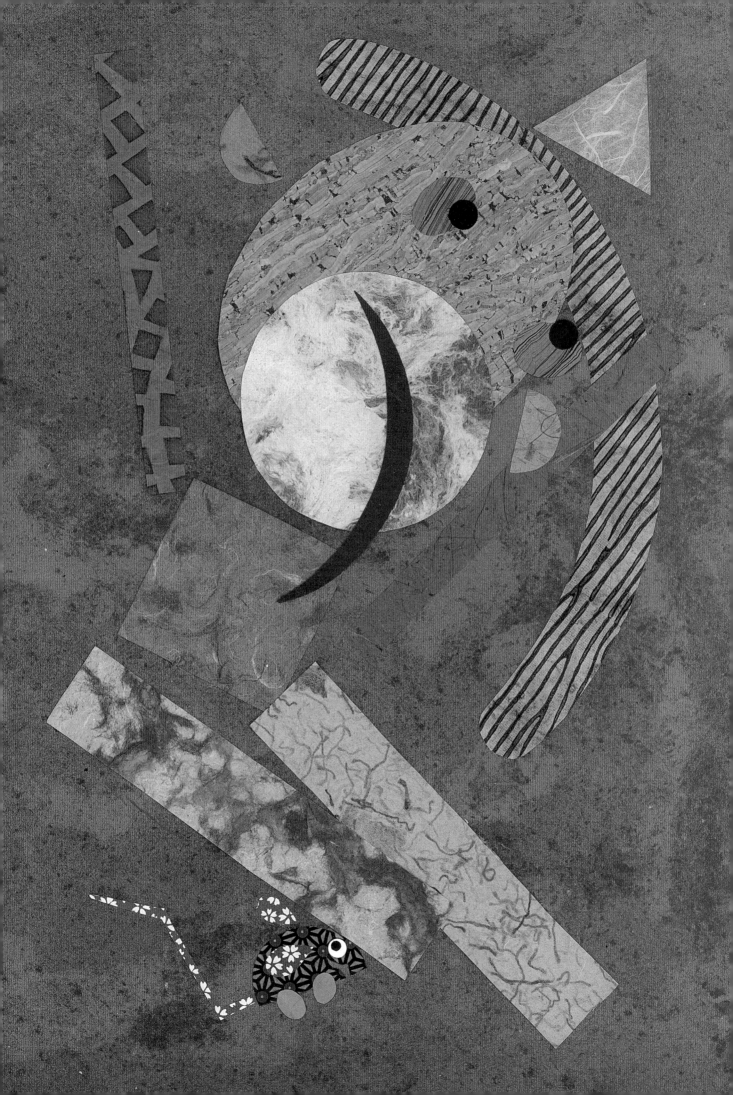

SHAPES, find your places!
It won't take long.

Go, SHAPES, go!
Wait . . .
something's wrong!

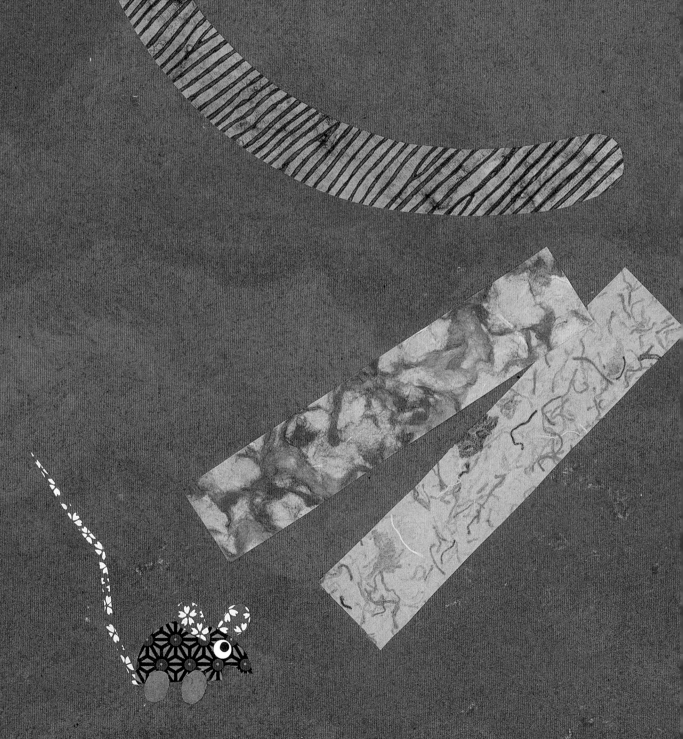

SHAPES,
oh SHAPES,

what have
you done?

No, SHAPES, no!
A cat's **no** *fun!*

I like MONKEYS.

Yes, I do.

I'll make a new monkey . . .

for me
and you.

Ta-da!